VIKING

Published by Penguin Group

Penguin Young Readers Group, 345 Hudson Street, New York, New York 10014, U.S.A.

Penguin Group (Canada), 90 Eglinton Avenue East, Suite 700, Toronto, Ontario, Canada
M4P 2Y3 (a division of Pearson Penguin Canada Inc.)

Penguin Books Ltd, Registered Offices: 80 Strand, London WC2R 0RL, England

First published in 2008 by Viking, a division of Penguin Young Readers Group

10   9   8   7   6   5   4   3   2   1

LIBRARY OF CONGRESS CATALOGING-IN-PUBLICATION DATA
Harrington, Janice N.
Roberto walks home/based on the characters created by Ezra Jack Keats;
written by Janice N. Harrington; illustrated by Jody Wheeler.
p.   cm.
Summary: Roberto is very angry when his older brother Miguel promises to walk him
 home from school and then forgets.
ISBN 978-0-670-06316-1 (hardcover)
[1. Brothers—Fiction. 2. Hispanic Americans—Fiction.] I. Keats, Ezra Jack.
II. Wheeler, Jody, ill. III. Title.
PZ7.H23815Ro 2008   [E]—dc22   2008011058

Manufactured in China   Set in Bembo

The illustrator would like to thank Laura Hart, Jill Macdonald, and Armani Spensieri,
for their valuable assistance in the creation of the artwork for this book, and Theo Simko
for his drawing on pages 20-21.

Roberto Walks Home

Story by Janice N. Harrington
Pictures by Jody Wheeler

Based on the characters created by

EZRA JACK KEATS

VIKING

Roberto waited.

He watched the other kids going home.

He watched the school buses come and go
like big yellow caterpillars.
But he waited.

He waved to Amy and her mother.

He waved to Susie and to his teachers.

"Aren't you walking home with us?" Peter asked.

"No," Roberto said. "My brother Miguel is coming. He promised
to walk me home today. We're going to play basketball."

Roberto waited.
He kicked his foot against the sidewalk.
He walked up the steps and down the steps.
He ran his fingers over the smooth, green leather
of the jacket that his brother had given him.

Roberto waited.
Waiting was hot and itchy.
Waiting was multiplication tables.
Waiting was looking up the street
and down the street.
Where was Miguel?

He slung the green leather jacket around his shoulders like a
cape and started home alone.
He walked past the yellow dog that growled *Rawww! Rawww!*
and threw itself at the fence.

He walked past the man pushing a grocery cart heaped with
plastic bags and dirty clothes.

He walked past the long dark alley soured with grease and garbage.

Roberto pushed his nose against the green jacket.

It smelled leathery. It smelled cinnamony, like Miguel.

He walked past the park where sometimes
Miguel played with him.
Roberto heard shouting and laughter.
He pushed his face against the fence.
He saw his brother shooting hoops
with the other big boys.

Sweat dripped from Miguel's face. He was laughing and hooting.
His feet moved double-quick, step-step-spin, stutter-step
and up into midair, like a bird.
Miguel sprang and shot the ball. *Whammmm*—it rang hard through
the rim. A big boy slapped Miguel's hands.
But Miguel did not see Roberto.
Roberto dropped the green leather jacket by the fence.
He didn't want it.

He hurried home and stomped up the stairs and slammed the door hard!

"Roberto, what's the racket?" his abuelo called.

Roberto did not answer. He jumped on his brother's bed.

Stomp! Stomp! Stomp!

He kicked Miguel's pillow on the floor.
He knocked down the tower he had built from blocks
and pushed his chair.
"Roberto-o-o."

"Sorry, Abuelo, sorry," Roberto called. But he wasn't.
He drew pictures of Miguel being chased by a yellow dog
and a basketball monster.
The dog wanted to bite him. The monster wanted to eat him.

"Help!" cried Miguel. "Help, Habichuelita!"
That's what Miguel called Roberto—Little Bean.
But now it was Miguel who was little.
Roberto drew him small, small, small.

Roberto stared out his window.

A pigeon sat on the fire escape.

It bobbed its head and looked at him.

It fluttered its wings and flew away.

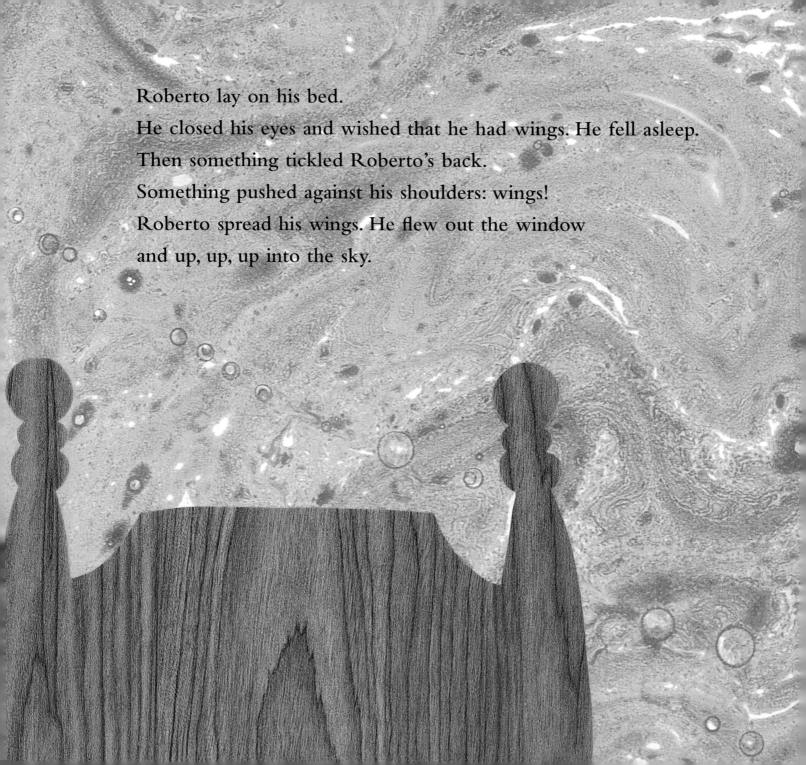

Roberto lay on his bed.

He closed his eyes and wished that he had wings. He fell asleep.

Then something tickled Roberto's back.

Something pushed against his shoulders: wings!

Roberto spread his wings. He flew out the window

and up, up, up into the sky.

He flew round and round and up and over and high.

He could see a woman walking dogs.

He could see the mailman going from door to door.

He saw his brother playing basketball far below.

Miguel shot the basketball.

It flew up, up, up and right into Roberto's hands.

Roberto laughed. He took the ball and flew away with it.

The big boys shouted and waved their arms.

They tried to run after him, but he flew too fast and too high.

"Habichuelita!" Miguel called.

But Roberto flew, higher than the hoop,
higher than the roofs and the trees,
higher than his big brother.

He wasn't a little brother anymore.
He wasn't Habichuelita.
He was a bird.

"Roberto . . . Habichuelita," Miguel said. "Wake up!
You want to shoot some hoops with me?"
Roberto opened his eyes.
His brother was standing beside his bed.
Roberto slid the covers over his head and turned away.
"Oh, Habichuelita . . . don't be that way," Miguel said.

"Go away. You're mean."
Roberto could feel his brother tugging the covers.
"I'm sorry, Roberto. . . . I'm sorry,
Habichuelita. I forgot, this time."
"But you promised me," Roberto whispered.

It was quiet. His brother didn't say anything.
Roberto turned to look, but Miguel had gone.
Beside the bed, he saw the green leather jacket,
and next to it he saw Miguel's basketball.
The basketball was Miguel's favorite thing.
It had Miguel's name on it.
He never let anyone borrow it.

Roberto found Miguel sitting on the stoop.

Miguel looked sad.

"Can we play for a long time?" Roberto asked.

"Till the moon is as big as a basketball,

Habichuelita!" Miguel said.

And they did.